LEONARD AND THE
CLOCKWORK FUTURE

Leonard and the Clockwork Future

Book 1

Lenny Leger

BOOK COVER BY LENNY LEGER USING COMPUTER ASSISTANCE

ILLUSTRATIONS BY LENNY LEGER USING COMPUTER ASSISTANCE

FIRST EDITION 2025

PRINTED IN THE UNITED STATES OF AMERICA

ISBN 979-8-9943591-0-5

THIS BOOK WAS TYPED IN APTOS AND GARAMOND

LEGER
PUBLISHING
& MEDIA

DEDICATION

To my mother who was always entertained by my stories about flying cars and the future.

And sheep.

TABLE OF CONTENTS

Forward

Time has always been a mirror; one that reflects not only where we are, but who we could have been.

When I began writing *Leonard and the Clockwork Future*, it wasn't simply about time travel or Tesla's lost inventions. It was about *what drives us to build machines that will alter time?*

Curiosity, ambition, love, or perhaps the quiet ache to set something right in the past.

Tesla dreamed of a world illuminated freely by the energy of the earth. In his vision, power and energy sources were not a commodity, but a birthright. I wondered what would happen if someone from our world—a century later, steeped in technology yet starved for meaning, created Tesla's universe.

That question became Dr. Leonard Vass. His journey is both scientific and spiritual: a man of equations learning that the universe is written not just in numbers, but in the harmonics of our hearts. Through him, I wanted to explore how invention and compassion are often two faces of the same spark of ambition.

This story is for those who tinker with lightning in the dark, the ones who chase impossible ideas, and those who still believe that the hum between seconds might hold something sacred.

For the daydreamers,
for the dream makers,
and for those who listen for the hum,
this book is for you.

— *Lenny Leger*

Preface

Leonard and the Clockwork Future started with one simple thought: What if I was stuck back in time and how would I get back?

Dr. Leonard Vass, a future quantum physicist obsessed with Nikola Tesla's forgotten work, spends years chasing the idea of Tesla's time machine that could bridge the gap between invention and destiny. Then one day, in a flash of miscalculated genius, he does it thus sending himself straight into 1909.

I wanted to write this story because I've always been drawn to that space of sci-fi becoming reality, where logic gives way to mystery, and the time-space continuum, Dr. Leonard's journey isn't just about time travel; it's about what happens when reason meets imagination, when progress meets compassion, and when a man realizes that changing the past might not be as important as understanding it.

For me, this story is a reminder that every person who's ever tried to make sense of the impossible shares something with Tesla, and perhaps, with Leonard too.

"We're all just trying to find our way back home, one day at a time." Lenny Leger

Introduction

History is not just a story written in stone.

It is a machine, a vast and intricate clockwork of gears and springs, where the removal of a single pin can change the turning of the world. It is a symphony of moments, each note dependent on the one that came before, and a change in a single chord can rewrite the entire melody.

And in every machine, there are ghosts. Echoes of what might have been. Whispers of forgotten geniuses, of futures that were promised but never delivered. What if you could hear those whispers? What if you could reach back through the turning gears and touch one of those ghosts?

But the machine of history is a jealous god. It does not like to be tampered with. To change the past is to risk the future. To save a hero is to risk becoming a ghost yourself. For every action, there is a reaction; for every rewritten past, there is an unforeseen consequence waiting in the wings.

This is a story of such a reach. A story of a man who stepped out of his time to touch a legend, and in doing so, set the clockwork of destiny on a new and dangerous course.

Turn the page and listen.

The gears are already turning.

Prologue

New York City, 1909

The fog came in off the East River that night like a ghost, a silent, gray thing that swallowed the gaslights and muffled the clatter of horse-drawn carriages until they were nothing but whispers and rumors.

It was a night for secrets, a night when the city itself seemed to hold its breath.

Inspector Welles felt the damp chill in his bones. He was a man of facts, of evidence, of things that could be measured, weighed, and filed away in a neat manila folder. He did not believe in ghosts.

But as he stood in the narrow, cobblestoned alley off Division Street, he felt the familiar, cold certainty of his world begin to fray at the edges.

There was no body. No blood. No signs of a struggle. There was only the object.

It lay in the center of the alley, nestled between the stones as if it had grown there. It was a small, smooth rectangle of the purest black he had ever seen, a piece of night that had fallen to earth.

It did not reflect the gaslight; it seemed to drink it.

Officer Malone, a good man with a simple mind, had been the first on the scene.

He wouldn't touch it.

"It... it hums, Inspector," Malone had stammered, his breath pluming in the cold air. "Not a sound you can hear, but one you can feel. In your teeth."

Welles knelt, his gloved hand hovering over the object. Malone was right. There was a vibration, a faint, impossibly high-frequency thrum that seemed to vibrate not in the air, but in the very space the object occupied. It was the feeling of a plucked string in a silent room, an echo of a note that had not yet been played.

He touched it. The cold was immediate, unnatural. It was not the cold of the November night; it was an absolute cold, a deep and profound absence of heat that felt ancient and alien. He picked it up. It had no weight to speak of.

It was like holding a piece of a shadow.

He turned it over in his hand. There were no seams, no maker's mark.

It was perfect, seamless, impossible. It was a thing that could not exist. And yet, here it was, lying in a dirty alley in the Lower East Side, humming a silent, secret song.

Inspector Welles slipped the object into his coat pocket. The unnatural cold seeped through the wool, a constant reminder against his side.

He did not know what it was, or where it had come from. He did not know that he was the first man in his time to hold a piece of the future.

He only knew that he had a new file to open, a new and impossible puzzle to solve.

And Inspector Welles always solved his puzzles.

The fog swirled around him, hiding the city, hiding the future, hiding everything but the cold, humming secret in his pocket.

Chapter 1

The Hum of Tomorrow

The year 2069 was a year of quiet brilliance, a time when humanity had finally outsmarted itself. Cities rose like polished circuitry from the green Florida landscape, glass and steel and light woven into silent, humming patterns. Drones whispered overhead, lazy as summer fireflies, their lights blinking in the warm, thick air. The world was a marvel of efficiency, a testament to a century of relentless progress. Still, it was a sterile kind of wonder. No one looked up at the sky anymore, for the sky had been charted, monetized, and photographed to death. The magic, it seemed, had been squeezed out of the world, leaving behind a beautiful, functional, and profoundly tired civilization.

Beneath the sprawling campus of the University of Central Florida, in a sub-basement sanctum that smelled of ozone and stale coffee, Dr. Leonard Vass was one of the last true believers. His laboratory was not the sterile white of the world above, but a place of controlled chaos, a cathedral of copper and shadow.

Coils of burnished metal, gleaming like ancient serpents, snaked along the walls, their curves echoing the silent, looping equations that danced on the quantum processors. The only constant sound was the rhythmic sigh of the air recycler, a sound like a sleeping giant, the sound of trapped genius.

On the far wall, a single photograph hung in a simple frame: a man with eyes that seemed to hold the storm, his gaze fixed on a future he had imagined but never reached.

A faded inscription in the corner read, *"To the future that will listen."* **Nikola Tesla.**

Leonard spoke to him sometimes, in the lonely hours before dawn, a quiet murmur of shared frustration and impossible dreams.

"We're close, old friend," he'd whisper, his breath fogging the cool glass of the frame. "The resonance, the frequency, the vibration... It's there. I can feel it."

Tonight, the hum in the lab was different. It was a deeper, more expectant thrum, a sound that seemed to vibrate not in the air, but in the bones. Leonard stood before the heart of his creation: a hybrid quantum coil, a shimmering nexus of plasma and light that pulsed with a soft, ethereal glow.

His hands, perpetually stained with the faint scent of ozone, moved with a surgeon's grace over the control panel, his fingers dancing a silent ballet of calibration and hope.

He was not alone. Dr. Mira Leung, a woman whose brilliance was a quiet flame to his raging fire, stood beside him. Her intelligence was like silk—soft, elegant, but unbreakable. She was his partner, in science and in the quiet spaces between the equations. Her presence was his anchor, the calm center to his storm of restless curiosity.

"The feedback loop is stabilizing," she said, her voice a low, melodic counterpoint to the machine's hum. "But the energy consumption is... astronomical, Leonard. It's drawing power from the entire campus grid."

Leonard didn't look away from the swirling plasma. "It needs it, Mira. To fold time, you need to borrow the energy of a star. Or at least, a city."

"And if you're wrong?" she asked, her hand resting gently on his arm.

Her touch was a question, a plea for him to remember the world outside this copper-lined tomb.

He turned to her then, his eyes, usually lost in the far distance of theoretical physics, focusing on her with a rare and startling intensity.

"Tesla wasn't wrong. He just ran out of time. He called it temporal resonance, a way of making two moments in history vibrate at the same frequency. Not a tunnel, not a brute force push, but a… a harmony."

He was a man who could speak to time but could never find the right words for the woman who loved him. He loved her, with a depth that frightened him, a love that felt as vast and unknown as the temporal equations he chased. But he was a man haunted by a ghost, a man who believed that the future was not something to be built, but something to be found, hidden in the lost whispers of the past.

"Just one more calibration," he said, his voice soft with a promise he wasn't sure he could keep. "I just need to align the plasma feedback. The resonance is unstable, it's… it's drifting."

Mira watched him, her heart a tangled knot of pride and fear. She believed in him, with a faith that defied the skepticism of their colleagues, the men who called him "Tesla's ghost."

But she also saw the exhaustion in the sharp lines of his face, the obsessive fire in his eyes. He was a man trying to outrun his own shadow, and she feared he was getting close to the edge.

He turned back to the machine, his fingers flying across the interface. The hum deepened, the light in the plasma coil brightening from a soft blue to an intense, blinding white. The air in the room grew thick, heavy, charged with an unseen energy. The copper coils on the walls began to glow with a faint, sympathetic light.

"Leonard…" Mira whispered, a sudden, cold dread washing over her.

A single, sharp alarm cut through the hum. A red light blinked on the console, a frantic, pulsing heartbeat in the growing storm of light and sound.

"Transfer Complete," the screen read, in stark, simple letters.

"Transfer of what?" Leonard murmured, his eyes wide with a mixture of terror and awe.

And then the world folded. It was not an explosion, but an implosion. A silent, violent folding of space and time, a soundless scream of reality turning in on itself. The room, the coils, the humming machines, all seemed to rush inward, collapsing into the blinding white light of the plasma core.

Leonard felt a sensation not of movement, but of being unwritten, of his very atoms being disassembled and re-tuned to a different, older song.

He saw a flash of Mira's face, her eyes wide with a love that transcended the collapsing reality around them. He reached for her, a desperate, silent cry, but his hand passed through empty air.

The world was gone.

There was a sound, then. A sound like the striking of a colossal bell, a sound that was both thunder and silence, a sound that echoed not in his ears, but in the very fabric of his being. And then, there was only darkness.

In the laboratory, in the quiet, sterile world of 2069, all that remained was the gentle sigh of the air recycler, the faint smell of ozone, and a single, blinking monitor.

The light from the plasma core had vanished, the hum had ceased.

But in the air, where the machine had stood, a faint, blue arc of electricity shimmered for a moment, a ghostly afterimage of a man who had loved the stars so much, he had forgotten to look at the people who lit his candles.

Then it, too, was gone.

The screen on the console still glowed, its message a silent, chilling epitaph:

"Transfer Complete."

Chapter 2

The City of Smoke and Sparks

He awoke to the scream of a steam whistle, the air dense with the smell of iron and coal. It was a thick, gritty film on his tongue, a taste so ancient and profound it felt like he had swallowed a piece of the earth itself. A cough rattled in his chest, a dry, hacking sound that sent a puff of black dust into the air.

He was lying on his side, his cheek pressed against something rough - cinders, he realized, still warm from a passing train. His body ached with a deep, resonant soreness, as if he had been struck by a bell and was still vibrating from the impact.

Slowly, Leonard pushed himself up, his limbs heavy and unresponsive. He was in a railway yard, a sprawling, skeletal landscape of iron tracks that gleamed like wet bones under a sky the color of dishwater. A locomotive, vast and black and breathing steam like a slumbering dragon, hissed on a nearby track.

The air was thick with a symphony of smells he had only ever read about in books: the sharp, metallic tang of hot iron, the acrid bite of coal smoke, the sweet, earthy scent of horses, and something else, something vaguely electric, the smell of a world just beginning to spark.

He rose unsteadily, wearing contemporary attire—a lightweight synthetic fabric intended for regulated environments that strikingly seemed insufficient and incongruous with his surroundings. A fine layer of soot covered him, a black baptism into this strange, new world.

He looked down at his hands, at the grime worked into the lines of his palms, and a wave of profound dislocation washed over him.

This was not his world.

This was not his time.

Panic, cold and sharp, began to prickle at the edges of his consciousness.

He fumbled in his pocket, his fingers searching for the familiar, smooth coolness of his digital interface. It was there, but it was wrong.

The device, usually warm and humming with latent energy, was cold and inert.

He pulled it out. The screen was dark, lifeless. He tried the activation sequence, his fingers tapping out the familiar code, but there was no response.

It was a dead thing, a beautiful, useless piece of glass and metal.

But then he felt it.

A faint, rhythmic pulse, a tiny, fading heartbeat in the palm of his hand. He turned the device over. The energy core, a sliver of contained quantum reality, continued to glow.

Still, its light was a weak, flickering blue, like a dying star. It was the only piece of his time that still lived, and it was fading fast.

"No," he whispered, the word a slight, lost sound in the vast, industrial roar of the yard. "No, no, no."

The city hummed and clattered and roared around him, a living, breathing entity of smoke and sparks. Men in dusty caps and heavy coats shouted in languages he barely recognized. Horses, their breath pluming in the cool air, pulled wagons over cobblestone streets that echoed with the clatter of iron-shod wheels.

And then he saw it—a sputtering, coughing automobile, a Model T, looking like an angry teapot on wheels, rattling past the entrance to the yard. Its sound was a mechanical novelty, a strange counterpoint to the familiar, organic rhythm of the horses.

He staggered out of the yard and onto the street, a ghost in a city of ghosts. The buildings climbed like proud, skeletal children, their steel frames reaching for a sky that seemed impossibly close. Electric lamps, their light a pale, uncertain yellow, buzzed and flickered, waging a losing war against the encroaching twilight.

A newsboy, his face smudged with ink and his voice a raw, hopeful cry, ran past, a stack of papers tucked under his arm.

Leonard caught a glimpse of the headline, a name that struck him like a physical blow: **"EDISON TRIUMPHS AGAIN!"**

Edison.

The name was a key, a turning point in the lock of his confusion. He looked around, his mind racing, piecing together the clues: the clothes, the cars, the gas lamps, the raw, untamed energy of the city.

He stumbled over to the newsboy, his hands trembling as he fumbled for a coin he didn't have.

"What… what year is it?" he asked, his voice hoarse.

The boy gave him a strange look, a mixture of pity and suspicion. "It's 1909, mister. You been on a bender?"

The year echoed in the silent chambers of Leonard's mind.

Not just any year. It was Tesla's last great year, the year he was still working in secret, the year before the world broke his heart and his spirit.
The year his own obsession was born.

The realization settled over him, not with a crash, but with a slow, cold dread. The machine hadn't just malfunctioned. It had worked.
It had tuned itself to the frequency of his own obsession, to the ghost he had been chasing his entire life, and it had sent him here.

To the source.

He was a man out of time, a man whose only connection to his own world was a dying pulse in his pocket. He was alone, in a city that was both beautiful and grim, a city that smelled of invention and despair. He was a hundred and sixty years from home, and the only man in the world who might understand, who might be able to help him, was a reclusive, disillusioned genius who was himself on the verge of being erased by the very world he had helped to build.

Nikola Tesla, the mad genius who created safe AC current, was shunned by Edison, who believed that direct current was the only way to power light bulbs. The same Tesla that invented the induction motor and radio, including remote controls, as well as fluorescent and neon lighting.

Leonard Vass, the man who had tried to conquer time, stood on a street corner in 1909, a lost soul in the age of smoke and sparks, and for the first time in his life, he was truly, utterly afraid. The city's heartbeat, a frantic, metallic rhythm, pulsed around him, and he felt like a single, discordant note in a symphony he could not comprehend.

The future was a distant, fading memory.

The past was a terrifying, tangible reality.

And he was trapped between them, a ghost in the machine of history itself.

Chapter 3

The Seamstress and the Stranger

He walked for hours, a ghost adrift on the currents of the city. His clothes, a marvel of nano-fabric and seamless design in his own time, were a costume of madness here. They clung to him, thin and strange, marking him as an outcast, a curiosity, a man who had fallen from some unseen, impossible place.

Men in bowler hats stared, their gazes lingering with a mixture of suspicion and contempt. Women pulled their children closer, their faces tight with a fear of the unknown. He was a ripple in the fabric of their reality, and the fabric was pushing back against him.

Every corner he turned, every street he crossed, was a fresh assault on his senses. The city was a relentless machine of life and death, of progress and decay. It was a world of sharp edges and soft, decaying corners, and he had no place in it.

The dying pulse of the energy core in his pocket was a constant, fading reminder of the world he had lost, a world of clean air and quiet efficiency, a world where he belonged.

Just as the last of the day's light began to bleed from the sky, painting the clouds in bruised shades of purple and orange, he found himself standing before a small shop, tucked between a boisterous pub and a silent, dark-windowed bakery.

The sign, painted in elegant but fading gold letters, read **"Abernathy & Son — Fine Tailoring."**

The "**& Son**" was ghosted, a pale whisper of a name that had long since departed. Through the window, he could see a single, warm light, a small, defiant star against the encroaching darkness. Inside, a woman sat bent over a sewing machine, her figure a silhouette of quiet, focused grace.

He didn't know why he chose that door. Perhaps it was the warmth of the light, or the quiet dignity of the sign, or perhaps it was simply that he had reached the end of his strength. He pushed the door open, a small bell announcing his arrival with a gentle, hesitant chime.

The woman looked up, her face framed by coils of silvering hair. Her eyes were the color of a winter sky, clear and sharp, yet they held a deep, quiet sadness —the look of a person who had learned to live with ghosts. She was perhaps fifty, her features soft but her posture straight, a woman held together by routine and propriety.

"Can I help you?" she asked, her voice brisk but not unkind. Her gaze took in his strange, soot-stained clothes, his wild hair, his eyes that seemed to hold a century of exhaustion. She did not gasp or recoil, but a flicker of cautious curiosity moved in her face.

Leonard's own voice, when it came, was a dry rasp. "I... I'm a professor," he began, the words feeling clumsy and false in his mouth. "There was an accident. A fire. I've lost... everything."

He gestured vaguely at himself, a man trying to explain a tear in the universe.

Mrs. Eleanor Abernathy had seen all manner of men in her shop. She had seen proud men and broken men, men in their Sunday best and men in their working rags. But she had never seen a man like this. He stood with a strange, straight posture, as if his bones were aligned to a different gravity.

His speech was too precise, too clean, the accent unplaceable. He looked less like a man who had survived a fire and more like a man who had fallen out of a storybook, a strange, sad creature from a land of impossible things.

She saw the desperation in his eyes, the profound, scholarly loneliness that clung to him like the soot on his clothes. She was a woman who knew loss, a woman whose own heart was a well of quiet grief.

She had lost her husband to a factory explosion, to the same kind of obsessive, dangerous work she now saw reflected in this stranger's eyes. She then decided on a small act of rebellion against the harshness of the world.

"You look like you could use a cup of tea," she said, her voice softening.

She gestured to a small, worn armchair in the corner.

"Sit. Rest a moment."

The simple kindness was his undoing. He sank into the chair, the springs groaning in protest, and a wave of gratitude so profound it bordered on pain washed over him.

The shop smelled of starch and lavender, with a faint, comforting scent of a coal stove. A tall clock ticked in the corner, its steady rhythm a small, mechanical heartbeat in the quiet room.

It was the sound of time.

Honest, tangible, and relentless.

As she prepared the tea, her sewing machine, a heavy, black iron beast, caught his eye. It was jammed, a tangle of thread caught in the mechanism.

He could see the problem instantly, a simple matter of friction and tension, a design flaw that a hundred years of progress had solved and forgotten. He stood and walked over to it, his fingers tracing the cold, iron body as if it were a living thing.

"Your machine," he said, his voice still rough. "It's… inefficient."

Mrs. Abernathy turned, a small, wry smile on her lips. "It's broken, professor. Like many things in this world."

"May I?" he asked, already reaching for the tangled thread. With a few deft movements, a twist of a screw, a slight adjustment to the tension spring, he cleared the jam. He found a small can of oil and applied a single, precise drop to a point of friction.

He turned the handwheel. The machine moved with a smooth, quiet grace it had not possessed in years.

Eleanor stared, her teacup halfway to her lips. It was a small thing, a simple repair, but he had done it with a certainty and an understanding that was… uncanny. It was as if he were not repairing the machine but reminding it of what it was supposed to be.

"How did you do that?" she whispered.

"I understand machines," he said simply. It was the truest thing he had said since he had arrived in this lost century.

In that moment, a connection was forged, a quiet, unspoken bond of mutual wonder. She saw past the strange clothes and the wild eyes to the brilliant, gentle soul beneath. He saw not just kindness, but acceptance, a safe harbor in the storm of the past.

He stayed. She gave him a plate of stew and a spare suit that had belonged to her late husband. It was heavy and scratchy and a size too big, but it was a uniform, a disguise. It made him feel a little less like a ghost.

"I must repay you," he said, his voice stronger now.

"You already have," she said, gesturing to the silent, repaired sewing machine. "But I can always use a hand with… the heavy work."

He needed a name.

"Leonard Vass" was a name from a future that no longer existed. He looked around the small, cluttered shop, his eyes landing on a slim volume of poetry on a nearby shelf. "The Poems of Arthur Vaughn."

"Vaughn," he said, testing the sound of it. "Leonard Vaughn. That's my name."

As he looked at his reflection in the dark shop window, a stranger in a dead man's clothes, he felt a flicker of something that was not quite hope, but a quiet resolve.

He was an alien in this world, but he was no longer alone.

The clock ticked on, each tick a second lost, a second gained.

He was a man out of time, and for the first time since he had arrived, he had found a small, quiet place to begin again.

The seamstress, the woman who smelled of lavender and starch, had stitched him into the fabric of 1909, and for now, it was enough.

It had to be.

Chapter 4

Sparks in the Alley

The city was a beast of hunger and invention, and Leonard, now cloaked in the borrowed identity of Leonard Vaughn, learned to feed it. He could not build a time machine out of spare parts and goodwill, not yet. He needed money, resources, and, most importantly, a way to navigate this world without revealing the impossible truth of his existence.

So he began to invent, not with the grand, sweeping gestures of his own time, but with the quiet, clever sparks of a man who could see the future in the gears of the present.

He started small. He took the simple, inefficient crystal radio sets being sold on street corners and, with a few deft touches—a tighter coil, a shard of silicon he'd painstakingly purified over a gas flame, a design whispered to him from a century away—he made them sing.

They became "**Vaughn's Whisper Boxes**," and they could pull voices from the air with a clarity that was unnerving, almost magical. He sold them not to the big department stores, but to small, curious shops in the city's teeming immigrant neighborhoods, places where the hunger for connection was a palpable, living thing.

Then came the "**Ever-Bright Filament**," a simple carbon-coated thread that made light bulbs burn twice as long and with a steadier, warmer light. He didn't sell the patent; he sold the process, teaching small, independent workshops how to create them, a quiet act of rebellion against the monolithic power of Edison's empire.

He was a ghost in the machine of the city's commerce, a whisper of a better, more efficient future.

Word began to spread.

Not in the bold headlines of the major papers, but in the back alleys and the smoky pubs, in the conversations of mechanics and tinkerers. They spoke of a strange, quiet man, the *"professor,"* who seemed to understand the secret language of machines. They called him the man who invented things no one had asked for, but everyone suddenly wanted.

His inventions were not revolutionary, not yet.

They were small miracles, quiet improvements in the noisy, clattering world of 1909.

It was through these small miracles that he met Eddie Rourke. Eddie was a boy of fourteen, though his eyes held the weary wisdom of a man twice his age. He was a creature of the city's streets, a newsboy and a shoeshine with a grin like a sparkplug and shoes two sizes too big. He moved through the city's veins like a vital pulse, hearing everything, seeing everything, and forgetting nothing.

Eddie found Leonard in a cold, damp workshop he had rented in a Brooklyn basement, a place that smelled of ozone and damp earth. Leonard was hunched over a new creation, a crude but functional motion detector, a device that would yelp with an electric buzz whenever something crossed its path.

Eddie had watched him for a week, a silent, curious shadow, before he finally spoke.

"What's that, mister?" he asked, his voice the raw, confident cry of a boy who had never known the luxury of fear.

Leonard looked up, startled. He saw a boy with a shock of red hair, a face smudged with the city's grime, and eyes that shone with an unquenchable curiosity. He saw a survivor.

"It's a watchdog," Leonard said, his voice soft. "An electric one."

Eddie's grin widened. "A watchdog that don't need to eat? You'll put every mutt in the city out of a job, Professor Future."

Professor Future.

The name stuck.

Eddie became Leonard's eyes and ears, his guide to the labyrinthine world of 1909. He ran messages, procured rare materials from scrapyards and back-alley dealers, and kept a watchful eye for anyone who showed too much interest in the strange man in the basement workshop. He became more than an ally; he became a friend, a small, bright spark of hope in the lonely darkness of the past.

It was Eddie who first brought him the name. He burst into the workshop one evening, his face flushed with excitement, a discarded newspaper clutched in his hand.

"Professor, you ain't the only ghost in this town," he said, spreading the paper on the workbench.

The article was a small, gossipy piece about the city's eccentrics. It mentioned a man who fed pigeons in the park, a man who claimed to speak to lightning, a man who lived in the opulent splendor of the Waldorf-Astoria but was rumored to be on the verge of ruin. A man named Nikola Tesla.

Leonard's heart hammered in his chest.
The Waldorf-Astoria.
He was here.
He was close.

The ghost he had been chasing his whole life was breathing the same smoky air, walking the same crowded streets.

"They say he's a madman now," Eddie said, his voice dropping to a conspiratorial whisper.

"That the big money men, the ones who own the whole damn city, they're done with him. They say he's being watched by thugs."

As if summoned by the words, a shadow fell across the basement window. Leonard looked up, his blood turning to ice. A black motorcar, sleek and silent as a shark, was parked across the street. Two men in long, dark coats stood beside it, their faces impassive, their eyes hidden in the shadows of their hats. They were not looking at the car, or at the street. They were looking at the workshop.

They were the men who built the century's bones and feared the soul that might inhabit it. They were the men who had funded Tesla and then abandoned him, the men who saw genius not as a gift, but as a commodity to be controlled or, if necessary, erased.

The Silver Circle.
The Investors Club.
Morgan. Rockefeller. Carnegie. Flagler.

Leonard knew, with the certainty that chilled him to the bone, that they were not watching for a forgotten madman. They were watching for the ripples he was creating, for the sparks of a future that was not their own. His small, quiet miracles had not gone unnoticed. The city's immune system was beginning to take note of the foreign body in its midst.

He was no longer just a lost man trying to find his way home. He was a player in a game he did not understand, a game whose rules were written in money and power. And the man who held the key to his own survival, the man in the grand hotel, was at the center of it all.

The black car pulled away, disappearing into the city's evening gloom, but the chill remained. The city was no longer just a place of wonder and disorientation. It was a place of danger. The hunt had begun.

Leonard looked at the newspaper, at the name of the man he had to find, and he knew that his time of hiding in the shadows was over.

He had to step into the light, even if it meant being seen by the men who owned the darkness.

Chapter 5

The Meeting of Two Men Out of Time

Getting to Tesla was like trying to book an audience with a king in a forgotten kingdom. The Waldorf-Astoria, a palace of glittering chandeliers and hushed carpets, was a fortress. Men in crisp uniforms guarded its entrances, their eyes trained to spot the unwanted, the impoverished, the eccentric. Leonard, with his growing reputation as the mysterious "Professor Vaughn," was all three.

His key came in the form of a man named Alistair Finch, a young, ambitious engineer for the city's burgeoning telephone network. Finch was captivated by Leonard's "***Whisper Box,***" and had sought him out, convinced he was a reclusive genius from Germany or Switzerland. For weeks, they had met in smoky cafes, Finch peppering Leonard with questions about resonance and frequency, Leonard answering with a frustrating, century-spanning vagueness.

"There's a man you must meet," Finch said one afternoon, his voice hushed with reverence. "The true master of the art. Nikola Tesla. He rarely sees anyone, but I'm installing a new internal telephone system for the hotel. I could get you in. Say you're a journalist, from… 'Scientific American.' He has a weakness for the press, especially if he thinks they'll finally listen."

The lie tasted like ash in Leonard's mouth, but he agreed. It was a flimsy key, but it was the only one he had.

A few days later, he was walking the plush corridors of the Waldorf-Astoria, his heart a frantic drum against his ribs. Finch led him not to a grand suite, but to a service entrance, and then down a flight of marble stairs into the hotel's humming underbelly. They stopped before a heavy oak door, unmarked and silent.

From beneath it leaked a faint, blue light and a smell like a coming storm.

"He calls it his workshop," Finch whispered, and knocked. "Wait here. And for God's sake, try not to upset him. He's… delicate."

The door opened a crack, and after a brief, murmured exchange, Finch was gone, leaving Leonard alone in the long, silent hallway. The door swung open.

The man who stood there was as tall and lean as a lightning rod, dressed in an impeccably tailored but slightly frayed suit. His face was a marvel of sharp, elegant planes, his mustache a dark, dramatic slash. But it was his eyes that held Leonard captive. They were the eyes of a man who had stared into the sun and argued with thunder, ancient and weary and burning with a fierce, unquenchable light. Nikola Tesla.

"The journalist," Tesla said, his voice a precise, melodic instrument with the cadence of a man who thought in a different language. He did not extend a hand.

He simply watched, his head tilted with the curiosity of a hawk studying a strange new creature in its domain.

He gestured for Leonard to enter. The room was not a room; it was a cathedral. It was a space of dim, reverent shadows and impossible light. Great copper coils, thick as a man's arm, snaked across the marble floor, their surfaces gleaming with a life of their own. Glass spheres and strange, metallic apparatus stood like silent, waiting acolytes.

The air was cool and thick with the smell of ozone, and high in the vaulted ceiling, pigeons cooed softly from the rafters, their gentle sounds a strange counterpoint to the low, electric hum that seemed to emanate from the very stones of the building.

As Leonard stepped across the threshold, something happened. The hum deepened. A series of vacuum tubes on a nearby table flickered, their filaments glowing with a sudden, sympathetic blue light.

The machines were reacting to him. To the dying energy core in his pocket.

It was a greeting.
A recognition.

Tesla's eyes narrowed. He saw it. He felt it. He closed the door, the sound; a heavy, final thud that sealed them in the electric darkness.

"You are no journalist," he said.

It was not a question.

"A journalist is a vessel for questions. You, sir, are an answer. You are a disruption in the frequency of things. I felt you long before you knocked on my door.
What are you?"

Leonard's carefully constructed lie crumbled into dust. He was in the presence of a mind that saw the world not as a collection of objects, but as a symphony of vibrations. To lie to this man would be like a single, discordant note trying to deny the existence of the orchestra.
"I am... a traveler," Leonard quietly stammered, his voice barely a whisper.

"Yes, we are all travelers," Tesla countered, his gaze unwavering. "But you... It seems you have traveled further than most. Your clothes are a lie. Your posture is a lie. Your name, I suspect, is a lie. But the science in your eyes... that is the only truth in this room besides my own."

There was no other way. Leonard reached into his pocket and pulled out the interface. The energy core, his last link to home, pulsed with a faint, dying light —a captured star in its final moments of life. He held it out, the strange, futuristic object looking alien and holy in the dim, electric light of the laboratory.

"This is who I am," Leonard said. "I am from a time that has not yet been born. A time that remembers you."

Tesla moved closer, his long, elegant fingers reaching out not for the device, but for the air around it. He did not touch it, but seemed to feel its energy, to read the story written in its quantum decay. He looked from the dying light in Leonard's hand to the burning exhaustion in Leonard's eyes.
He saw the impossible truth.

He did not laugh.
He did not recoil.
A profound, weary sadness seemed to settle over his features, the look of a man who had always known he was born in the wrong century and had just been handed the proof.

He walked over to a large blackboard covered in a cascade of chalk equations, a waterfall of frozen lightning. He picked up a piece of chalk and, with a soft, scratching sound, wrote a single, elegant formula.

As he turned back to Leonard, a strange, sad smile playing on his lips. He tapped the equation on the board.

"Time," he said, his voice as soft as falling dust, "is a form of energy. And energy, like a river, can be diverted. I have always known this. The world has labeled me as a madman for it."

He glanced at the fading light in Leonard's hand, and then back at Leonard himself; the smile slowly faded, replaced by a look of profound understanding.

He saw not a madman, but a fellow traveler, a fellow ghost.

"Then perhaps time," Tesla said, his voice dropping to a whisper that was both a conclusion and a prayer, "like electricity, only awaits the correct conductor."

In that moment, the hundred and sixty years that separated them collapsed into nothing. They were two men out of time, two geniuses who had been cursed with the loneliness of seeing too much.

The inventor who had dreamed of the future, and the man who had come back to find him. The air in the room hummed with a new kind of energy, a new frequency.

A frequency of hope.

Chapter 6

The Silver Circle

While hope was being forged in the electric cathedral beneath the Waldorf-Astoria, a different kind of power was being brokered in a smoky, mahogany-paneled room many miles away. This was the world of the Silver Circle, a gentlemen's club so exclusive and so powerful that its members did not simply influence the world; they owned the patent on it. In a room that smelled of imported cigars, musky leather, and the stale odor of persistence, the gods of the Gilded Age gathered to cast their lots.

John D. Rockefeller, a man whose face seemed carved from granite and piety, sat like a silent, brooding monarch. J.P. Morgan, with his fierce, burning eyes and a bulbous nose that seemed to cleave the air before him, radiated a restless, predatory energy. Andrew Carnegie, smaller and bird-like in stature, watched with shrewd, calculating eyes, a man who had built an empire on steel and was now trying to build a legacy on philanthropy, a final, desperate hedge against the judgment of history. And Henry Flagler, the sun-bronzed, shoe-bristle mustached emperor of Florida, a man who had painted a railway paradise onto a swamp, sat with a quiet, reptilian stillness.

They were the men who had built the century's bones, but they feared the soul that might inhabit it. They spoke in a kind of poetry, a language of capital and control, poetry poisoned by greed.

Tonight, they gathered; their conversation was a low, dangerous murmur, and the subject was a ghost they thought they had long since buried: Nikola Tesla.

"He is a liability," Morgan growled, his voice a low rumble of thunder. "A poet in a world that requires plumbers. We funded his dreams of free energy, and he gave us… pigeons and lightning storms.

Now, I hear whispers. He has a new acolyte. A mysterious inventor who appears from nowhere, creating trifles that are just a little too clever."

"Vaughn," Flagler said, his voice a dry rustle.

"My men here in New York have been watching him. He's a strange one, indeed. No history. No connections. He creates small, efficient miracles and gives them away.

It's unnatural. It's… inefficient."

"It's the same disease," Rockefeller said, his voice thin and sharp as a cobbler's tack. "The disease of progress without profit. It is a dangerous sentiment. It is the sentiment of anarchists and fools. Tesla was its prophet. This new man, this 'Vaughn,' sounds like his disciple."

Carnegie shifted in his leather chair. "Perhaps we are being too hasty. The man's inventions are harmless.

Light bulbs that last longer? Radios that are clearer? These are not threats. They are… improvements."

Morgan slammed his fist on the mahogany table, making the crystal glasses tremble. "Improvements are a threat! Our empires are built on the planned obsolescence of the present. On the promise of a future that we control, that we sell, piece by piece. This Vaughn, this ghost, is giving away the future for free. And he is doing it in Tesla's shadow. What do you think they are building down there, in that basement laboratory of his? A better mousetrap? I think not. I think they are building a weapon. A weapon that could rewrite the rules."

"If we can't buy time," Morgan said, his voice dropping to a low, menacing whisper, "we'll buy the men who invent it. And if we cannot buy them, we will break them."

Into this circle of smoke and power, a man was summoned. Inspector Welles was a man of devout, unshakable rationality. He was stocky, dressed in a simple, dark suit, his face a mask of stern, professional calm. He was a man who believed in order, in facts, in reports filed in triplicate. He did not believe in ghosts.

"Inspector," Flagler said, his voice smooth as oil. "We have a matter of… national interest. A potential threat. A scientific anarchist and his new, impressionable student. We need to know what they are building. We need to know if they are a danger to the established order of things."

Welles listened, his face impassive. He secretly admired Tesla, the sheer, mad audacity of the man's vision. But he also believed that men like Tesla invited chaos. They were sparks in a world built of tinder. His job was to extinguish the sparks.

"I will look into it," Welles said, his voice as dry as a legal document. "I will file a report."

As he left the room, the men of the Silver Circle returned to their cigars and brandy, confident that the problem was being handled, that the machine of the world they had built would grind on, undisturbed.

They did not see the small, grimy face pressed against the foggy window of the alleyway, the face of a boy with shoes two sizes too big and eyes that missed nothing. Eddie Rourke had followed the black motorcars here, a small, invisible shadow in their wake. He could not hear the words, but he could read the language of power in the grim faces, in the angry gestures. He saw Inspector Welles leave, and he knew, with the unerring instinct of the streets, that the man was a hunter.

He ran.

He ran through the labyrinth of the city's back alleys, his heart a frantic drum against his ribs. He ran to the basement workshop where a man from the future was trying to build a bridge home. He burst through the door, his breath coming in ragged gasps, his face pale with a fear that was not for himself.

"Professor," he panted, leaning against the doorframe. "The men…. In the black cars… They're not just watching anymore…. They've sent a hunter."

Leonard looked up from the delicate, intricate work of weaving his own quantum mechanics into the beautiful, brutalist coils of Tesla's design. The chill he had felt outside his workshop weeks ago returned, colder and sharper now. The city was no longer just watching.

It was closing in.

The ghosts of the past and the hunters of the present converged on the small, electric cathedral, where two men were trying to teach time a new song.

And Leonard knew, with a sudden, terrible clarity, that the song might be a requiem.

Chapter 7

Copper and Candlelight

The days that followed were a strange and beautiful dream, a symphony of copper and candlelight, of rustling blueprints and the low, constant hum of impossible physics. The hunt was on, the city was closing in, but within the walls of Tesla's subterranean laboratory, time itself seemed to slow, to bend to the will of the two men who were trying to unravel its secrets. They worked with quiet, desperate urgency, a silent understanding passing between them — the man from the future and the man who had dreamed it.

It was a collaboration that was pure poetry.

Tesla, with his long, elegant fingers and his mind that saw the universe as a series of beautiful, resonant waves, would sketch by the flickering light of a candle, his chalk whispering across the blackboard, his designs a magnificent, baroque fusion of art and science.

He worked with the raw, untamed power of his own time, with massive coils and brutal, beautiful arcs of lightning. He spoke of frequencies and harmonics, of resonance across time, of tuning the world as one would tune a violin.

Leonard, in turn, would sit by the soft, steady glow of a bare electric lamp, his own world's equations a quiet, elegant counterpoint to Tesla's grand, sweeping visions. He worked with the hope in his pocket, the dying energy core, carefully extracting its secrets, its quantum language.

He spoke of folded space, of plasma feedback loops, of the digital soul of his own century. He was the phantom in Tesla's machine, the whisper of a future that had already come to pass.

They were two halves of a single, brilliant mind, separated by a century of progress and pain. Leonard would watch, mesmerized, as Tesla would coax a ball of lightning into existence, holding it in his bare hands, a captured star, a piece of the sun brought down to earth.

And Tesla would listen, his ancient eyes wide with childlike wonder, as Leonard explained the impossible logic of quantum entanglement, particles that could communicate with each other across the void of space and time.

"You see with a clarity that is both a blessing and a curse," Tesla told him one night, his voice soft in the humming darkness. "You have seen the end of the song. I have only ever been able to hear the first few notes."

Into this world of electric dreams and quiet desperation, a new, gentle rhythm was introduced.

Mrs. Eleanor Abernathy, the seamstress who had stitched Leonard into the fabric of her world, began to visit. She would arrive each evening, a small basket on her arm, her presence a quiet, grounding force in the storm of their work.

She would bring them plates of warm stew, fresh bread, and hot, sweet tea. She was the warmth of the century he had landed in, and the reason he was beginning to forget why he had to leave.

Eleanor would sit in a small wooden chair in the corner of the laboratory, her knitting needles clicking softly, a steady, rhythmic counterpoint to the hum of the machines. She did not understand their work in the same way they did.

But Mrs. Abernathy understood the passion, the fire, the dangerous, beautiful obsession that drove them as she had seen it before, in the eyes of her late husband. But here, in this strange, electric cathedral, it felt different.

It felt less like a path to ruin and more like a prayer.

She and Leonard rarely spoke of anything important. Mostly small talk. They spoke of the weather, of the price of bread, of the strange, new moving pictures that were beginning to appear in the city.

But in the quiet spaces between the words, something grew. A look, a shared smile, the way his hand would brush against hers as he took a plate of food. It was a gentle, aching affection, a love that could never be spoken, for it was a love that belonged to two different worlds, two different times.

She saw the loneliness in him, the profound, unbridgeable gulf that separated him from everyone around him. And he saw in her a strength and a kindness that felt more real, more tangible, than any of the sterile wonders of his own time. She was the soul of a century that never wrote equations, only letters that smelled of dust and rain. And he was falling in love with her.

One evening, as a cold, autumn rain lashed against the city streets above, they achieved their first minor miracle. They had completed the primary coil, a beautiful, intricate fusion of Tesla's massive copper windings and Leonard's delicate, quantum-laced filaments. The dying energy core was nestled in its heart, a faint, blue jewel in a nest of lightning.

"It is time," Tesla said, his voice trembling with a mixture of excitement and fear.

Leonard nodded, his own heart hammering. He made the final connection. The hum in the room deepened, its pitch rising to become a clear, resonant tone. The air grew thick, shimmering, as if the heat of a summer day had been trapped in the room. The light from the core brightened, pulsing in time with the hum.

And then, for a single, breathtaking moment, the world bent. A small, silver wrench, lying on the workbench a few feet away, lifted into the air, hovered for a moment in the shimmering, distorted space, and then vanished.

It did not fall.
It did not fly.
It simply ceased to be.

A moment later, the hum faded, the light dimmed, and the air in the room returned to normal. The wrench was gone.

Tesla and Leonard stared at the empty space on the workbench, their faces pale in the dim light. Eleanor had risen to her feet, her knitting forgotten in her lap, her eyes wide with a silent, profound awe.

"The resonance," Leonard whispered, his voice choked with emotion. "It's stable. We found the frequency."

Tesla reached out and placed a hand on Leonard's shoulder, his grip surprisingly strong. There were tears in his ancient, weary eyes.

"You have conducted the orchestra, my friend from tomorrow," he said, his voice thick with a lifetime of vindication. "You have made time itself sing."

In the corner, Eleanor Abernathy smiled, a quiet, secret smile. She did not understand the science, but she understood the music. And it was the most beautiful, hopeful sound she had ever heard.

The wrench was gone, but something new had appeared in the room, something bright and fragile and full of an impossible light.

It was the future.

And for the first time, it felt within their reach.

Chapter 8

The Raid

The moment of triumph was a fragile, shimmering bubble, and it was destined to burst. The beautiful, impossible note they had struck hung in the air for a heartbeat, a promise of a future they might yet build. But the world outside, the world of iron and greed and men who feared the songs they could not own, was already moving to silence it.

The first sign was a sudden, sharp silence from above. The distant, familiar rumble of the city, the clatter of wagons, the cry of vendors, the low hum of a world in motion—was abruptly cut off. It was replaced by a heavy, expectant stillness, the kind of quiet that precedes a storm.

Then came the sound. A heavy, rhythmic booming on the service door at the end of the hall, a sound like the fist of a giant. It was a sound that had no place in the hushed, elegant world of the Waldorf-Astoria. It was the sound of brute force, of an order that had no time for politeness.

Tesla's face, which had been alight with a joy that had made him look young again, went pale. The light in his eyes flickered and died, replaced by a familiar, weary resignation.

"They have come," he said, his voice a flat, dead thing. "The men who wish to put the lightning back in the bottle."

Leonard's blood ran cold. He looked at the machine, the beautiful, intricate heart of his hope, now vulnerable and exposed. He thought of the dying core, his last, fragile link to Mira, to his own time.

They were so close. They just needed more time.

Before they could move, the oak door to the laboratory, the door that had sealed them in their electric sanctuary, splintered and burst inward. The figures that filled the doorway were not the dark-coated goons of the Silver Circle. They were worse. They were men in the blue uniforms of the city police, their faces grim and impassive, their movements efficient and cold. And leading them, his face a mask of stern, reluctant duty, was Inspector Welles.

"Nikola Tesla," Welles announced, his voice echoing in the sudden, shocked silence of the cathedral of coils. "You are under arrest. By the authority of the United States government, on suspicion of espionage and conducting experiments prejudicial to the national interest."

Espionage.

The word was a lie, a convenient, brutal weapon. It was the charge they leveled at men whose ideas were too big, too dangerous, for the small minds who ran the world.

Tesla did not resist. He seemed to shrink into himself, the tall, proud lightning rod of a man suddenly stooped and frail.

He looked at his beautiful machines, his captured lightning, his cooing pigeons in the rafters, and a look of profound, heartbreaking sorrow passed over his face. It was the look of a king being exiled from his own kingdom.

As the officers moved to flank him, Welles's gaze fell upon Leonard. "And you, sir. I do not know who you are, but you are a person of interest. You will come with us."

Panic, sharp and blinding, seized Leonard. He couldn't be taken. To be taken was to lose everything. The machine, the core, the last, fading hope of home. He backed away, his eyes darting around the room, searching for an escape that didn't exist.

And then, a sound. A high, sharp whistle from the hallway, three short bursts.

Eddie.
He was out there.
He had seen them coming.

The whistle was a trigger. In the confusion, as two officers moved to grab the unresisting Tesla, a small, dark shape darted from behind a massive coil. It was Eddie Rourke, his face a pale, determined smudge in the dim light. He was holding a small, round object in his hand.

"Professor, run!" he yelled, and with a surprising strength, he hurled the object at a bank of glass vacuum tubes on the far wall. It was one of Tesla's own creations, a small, volatile sphere of compressed gas.

The sphere shattered against the tubes, and the world erupted in a flash of blinding white light and a deafening roar. The air was filled with a shower of sparks and the sharp, acrid smell of ozone.

The lights in the laboratory flickered and died, plunging the room into a chaotic twilight, lit only by the faint, pulsing blue of the time machine's core.

In the chaos, Leonard felt a small, strong hand grab his.

"This way!" Eddie hissed, pulling him toward a dark, narrow opening in the wall, a service tunnel Leonard had never known existed.

Leonard hesitated, his eyes fixed on Tesla. The old man was being led away, a ghost in the custody of lesser men. Their eyes met for a fleeting second across the chaotic, spark-filled room. Tesla gave a slight, almost imperceptible nod, a silent command.

Go. Survive.

Then he was gone.

Eddie pulled him into the darkness of the tunnel just as Welles's voice cut through the ringing in his ears.

"Stop him! Do not let him escape!"

But it was too late. They were in the hotel's guts, a labyrinth of pipes and wires. As they scrambled through the darkness, a new sound reached them from the laboratory behind, a sound of brutal, senseless destruction. The sound of heavy hammers smashing delicate glass, of iron bars tearing through copper coils.

They were destroying it. They were killing his hope.

A final, sickening crash, followed by a fizzing, dying hum, and the faint blue light that had been spilling into the tunnel from the lab was extinguished.

The core. They had smashed the core.

Leonard cried out, a raw, wounded sound. The last light from his own time, the last whisper of Mira's world, had been snuffed out. He stumbled, his strength gone, his body wracked with a grief so profound it felt like a physical blow.

Eddie held him up. "Come on, Professor!" the boy urged, his voice tight with fear. "We gotta go. We can't stop now."

He was right. To stop was to be caught, to be erased. Leonard let the boy pull him through the darkness, his mind a numb, echoing void. They emerged into a cold, rain-swept alley, the city's noise a shocking, brutal roar after the silence of the tunnels.

They didn't stop running. They ran until their lungs burned and their legs ached, until the sounds of pursuit had faded, until they were lost in the anonymous, teeming streets of the city.

They found refuge in the cold, damp emptiness of Leonard's basement workshop, the place where his small miracles had been born.

Leonard sank to the floor, the full weight of the disaster crushing him. Tesla was gone. The machine was a wreck of shattered glass and broken wire. And the core… he reached into his pocket. His fingers closed around the familiar shape of the interface, but the faint, comforting pulse was gone. He pulled it out. The sliver of quantum reality, the heart of his machine, was dark.

Not a dying blue, but a dead, final black.
It was over.
Time, for Leonard Vass, was running out.

It had, in fact, already run out. He was marooned, a man without a past, without a future, a ghost in a city that had just declared war on him. And the only man who could have helped him was lost in the very darkness they had tried to illuminate. The raid was over, but the true desperation had just begun.

Chapter 9

The Clockwork Betrayal

Desperation is a cold, hollow room, and in the days that followed the raid, Leonard lived in its deepest chamber. The silence from his pocket was a constant, screaming void. The dead energy core was a piece of his own soul that had been ripped out, leaving a wound that would not heal. He was no longer just a man out of time; he was a man running on borrowed time, and the clock was ticking with a terrifying, final rhythm.

He had to rebuild. The thought was a madness, a fool's errand, but it was the only thing that stood between him and the abyss. He haunted the scrapyards and the junk heaps of the city, a gaunt, haunted figure in a borrowed coat, searching for the raw materials of a miracle. He needed copper, glass, and wire, but more than that, he needed power. A lot of it. The kind of power that could only be bought with money.

And so, he began to sell his soul, piece by piece. He took the small, clever inventions that had once been his pride, his quiet acts of rebellion, and he sold them to the highest bidder. He sold them to men with greedy eyes and slick smiles, men who saw his genius not as a gift, but as a weakness to be exploited. One of these men was Harold "Hal" Bixby.

Bixby was an inventor and a patent broker, a man who was part opportunist, part dreamer, with a grin that was all business.

He had a gold tooth that flashed when he lied, which was often. He saw the desperation in Leonard's eyes, the frantic, brilliant energy, and he smelled profit. He befriended Leonard, offering him resources, contacts, and a sympathetic ear.

At the same time, his mind calculated the value of the secrets hidden behind the professor's haunted eyes.

"You're a man of vision, Leonard," Bixby would say, his hand clapping Leonard's shoulder with a false familiarity. "But you're no businessman. You need a partner. Someone to handle the… practical side of things."

Leonard, lost in his grief and his obsession, trusted him. He gave Bixby the designs for his **"Ever-Bright Filament,"** his **"Whisper Box,"** and even the crude but effective motion detector that had once guarded his workshop. Bixby promised him the world. He gave him a pittance, just enough to buy the copper and the wire for a new, smaller, more desperate machine.

And then, betrayed him. He sold the designs not to workshops, but to the very men who were hunting Leonard. He sold them to an intermediary for the Silver Circle.

It was Eleanor Abernathy who discovered the betrayal. She had become Leonard's silent, watchful guardian. She saw the darkness gathering around him, the way the light in his eyes was dimming, the way he was being consumed by his hopeless quest.

One evening, she saw him with Bixby in a smoky pub, saw the flash of the gold tooth, the predatory gleam in the broker's eyes, the sheaf of papers passing between them.

She knew the look of a shark. She had seen it in the eyes of the men who had owned the factory where her husband had died.

She followed Bixby. She saw him meet with a man in a dark coat and a fine hat, a man who had the cold, impassive look of a Silver Circle agent. She saw the designs, Leonard's beautiful, intricate drawings, exchanged for a thick envelope of cash. The clockwork of the city, the gears of greed and power, were grinding her friend into dust.

That night, she came to the workshop. The new machine was a skeletal, pathetic thing compared to the grand cathedral of coils in Tesla's lab. It was a machine born of desperation, built in a cold, damp basement, powered by a grief that was rapidly turning to madness.

Leonard was hunched over it, his hands trembling, his face pale and gaunt in the dim light. He looked up as she entered, his eyes wild and lost.

"It's not enough," he whispered, his voice a dry, rattling thing. "The power source… it's dead. It's all dead."

Eleanor walked over to him, her heart aching at the sight of this brilliant, broken man. She placed a hand on his arm. "Leonard," she said, her voice soft but firm. "You have to stop. This will kill you."

"I can't stop," he cried, his voice breaking. "Don't you understand? I'm not from here. I'm from another time. I have to go back. I have to get home."

The secret was out, hanging in the cold, damp air between them. He expected her to recoil, to call him a madman, to run. But she did not. She simply looked at him, her eyes full of a sad, profound understanding.

"I know," she whispered. "I've known for a long time. No man from this time has eyes like yours, Leonard. You look at the world as if you're remembering it."

In that moment, the last of his defenses crumbled. He buried his face in his hands and wept, the silent, racking sobs of a man who had lost everything. She held him, her arm was a warm, safe harbor in the storm of his grief. She was the anchor he had not known he needed, the quiet, steady heartbeat in the chaos of his collapsing world.

From that night on, she was his partner. She used the small savings she had, the money she had put aside for a future that no longer held any promise, and she helped him. She smuggled materials to the workshop, hiding them in bolts of cloth and laundry baskets. She stood watch, her quiet presence a shield against the hostile world outside.

Their unspoken affection blossomed in the dim light of the workshop, a fragile, impossible flower growing in the ruins of his hope. It was a love that could never be, a love that was as beautiful and as tragic as a sunset.

One evening, as she was mending the lining of the old, borrowed coat he wore, her fingers found something hidden in the seam. A small, flat object wrapped in oilcloth. It was a piece of a blueprint, a fragment from the raid, that must have been torn off and somehow ended up in his pocket. She gave it to him.

Leonard unwrapped it. It was a section of Tesla's design for the primary coil, but there was something else. Scrawled in the margin, in Tesla's elegant, familiar handwriting, was a message —a secret whispered across the void of their separation.

It was not a formula. It was a line of poetry.

"Frequency is memory. Follow the light."

Leonard stared at the words, his heart pounding. It was a code. A clue. A final gift from the master.

Frequency is memory.

He had been so focused on the machine, on the hardware, on the dead power source. He had been trying to rebuild the instrument. But Tesla was telling him that the music was not in the instrument.

It was *in* the musician.

Follow the light...

What light?

The core was dead.
There was no light.

He looked up, his eyes meeting Eleanor's. She was watching him, her face full of a quiet, unwavering faith. And in that moment, he understood. The light was not in the machine. It was in the love, the trust, the human connection that had saved him from the darkness. It was in the quiet courage of a newsboy, the grudging respect of a weary inspector, the gentle, impossible love of a seamstress from another time.

He did not need to rebuild the power source. He was the power source. His own temporal frequency, his own memory of the future, that was the key. The machine was not a vehicle. It was an antenna. An amplifier for the song that was already inside him.

A new kind of hope, fragile but fierce, began to dawn in the cold, hollow room of his heart. The betrayal of Hal Bixby had almost destroyed him. But the quiet, unwavering faith of Eleanor Abernathy had saved him.

The clockwork of the city was still turning against him, but he now had a secret of his own. A secret whispered to him by a ghost, a secret that might just be enough to get him home.

The game had changed.
And he was finally ready to play.

Chapter 10

The Storm Gathers

The city held its breath. A strange, electric tension settled over the streets, a low hum that had nothing to do with Tesla's coils or Leonard's desperate machine. It was the tension of a coming storm, a real one, a monster of wind and rain that was gathering its strength out over the gray, churning Atlantic. The sky was a bruised, swollen lid, pressing down on the city, and the air was thick with the smell of ozone and wet earth. The weather was turning, and with it, the tides of fate.

In the damp basement workshop, Leonard worked with a newfound clarity. Tesla's cryptic message had unlocked a door in his mind. Frequency is memory. He was the tuning fork, the resonant core. The machine he was building was no longer a vehicle, but an amplifier, a way to broadcast the unique temporal signature of his own being, to make the universe hear his song of displacement and longing.

He worked with a quiet, feverish intensity, his hands steady, his mind sharp. The skeletal machine began to take on a new, strange beauty. It was a harp of copper and glass, designed not to travel, but to sing. To sing a single, perfect, resonant note that would echo back to the future he had lost.

Outside, the other storm was gathering. Inspector Welles, a man haunted by the impossible things he had seen in Tesla's lab, was closing in. He was a good man, a man who believed in order, but the order of his world had been shattered. He was a skeptic who had stared too long into the aurora and had begun to believe. He did not want to hunt Leonard, but it was his job. The Silver Circle, the faceless men of money and power, were demanding results. They wanted the ghost in the machine captured, dissected, and neutralized.

Eddie Rourke, the city's small, loyal heartbeat, was a shadow in the streets, his eyes and ears tuned to the whispers of the hunt. He saw the plain-clothed officers, the dark cars lingering on street corners, the net that was slowly, inexorably tightening around the Brooklyn neighborhood where Leonard was hidden. He was a boy playing a man's game, a dangerous game of hide-and-seek with men who did not play fair.

He was nearly caught once, cornered in an alley by two of the Silver Circle's goons, men with eyes like typewriter keys and hands that looked like they were made of stone. He escaped by diving into a sewer grate, the laughter of the men echoing in the darkness behind him.

He brought the news to the workshop, his face pale, his clothes reeking of the city's underbelly.

"They're close, Professor," he whispered, his voice trembling. "They're on this street. They're asking questions."

Leonard looked at the sky through the small, grimy basement window. The clouds were a churning, angry sea of black and gray. The storm was almost here. It was now or never.

That evening, as the first drops of rain began to fall, fat and heavy as coins, Eleanor came to the workshop for the last time.

She carried a small, carefully wrapped package. She did not speak of the danger, of the men who were closing in. She spoke only of the storm.

"It will be a bad one," she said, her voice quiet and steady, a calm center in the growing storm inside and out. "The kind of storm that washes the world clean."

She handed him the package. He unwrapped it. It was the coat, the old, borrowed suit coat that had belonged to her husband. But it changed. She had spent the last few days working on it, her needle flying, her heart aching with a love she could not speak.

She had lined the entire coat with a fine, intricate mesh of copper thread, a beautiful, shimmering web woven into the dark fabric. It was a work of art, a labor of love, a shield against a world she did not understand.

"For your journey," she said, her voice catching on the words. "So you do not travel alone."

Leonard looked at the coat, at the thousand tiny stitches, each one a prayer, a tear, a silent goodbye. He understood. It was more than a gift. It was a component. An antenna. A way of wrapping himself in the very fabric of the machine, of making himself the heart of the circuit. It was the final piece of the puzzle.

He put it on. It was heavy, alive, humming with a faint, latent energy. It fit him perfectly.

He turned to her, and in the dim light of the workshop, in the quiet moments before the end of the world, he finally said the words that had been caught in his throat for weeks.

"Eleanor," he began, his voice thick with an emotion he could no longer contain. "I…"

She placed a finger on his lips, her eyes shining with unshed tears. "I know," she whispered. "Go. Go home, Leonard. Find your own time. Find your Mira."

It was a gift of impossible generosity, a love so pure it was willing to let him go, to erase itself for the sake of his happiness. He looked at this woman, this seamstress who had stitched his broken soul back together, and he knew that he would carry the memory of her, the scent of lavender and starch, the quiet courage in her eyes, across a hundred years of time.

He kissed her then, a gentle, desperate kiss that was both a beginning and an end, a promise and a farewell. It was a kiss that tasted of salt and rain and the impossible, tragic beauty of a love that could never be.

Outside, the sky split open. A jagged fork of lightning tore through the darkness, followed a moment later by a deafening crash of thunder. The storm had arrived.

The final act had begun.

The city and the heavens held their breath, waiting for the man from the future to make his last, desperate stand.

Chapter 11

Thunder and Light

The storm broke over the city with a biblical fury. Rain fell in solid, wind-driven sheets, turning the streets into dark, churning rivers. The sky was a canvas of continuous, silent lightning, the world flickering between moments of stark, brilliant clarity and profound, absolute darkness. And then the thunder, a rolling, apocalyptic cannonade that shook the very bones of the city. It was the sound of the world ending, or beginning.

Down in the basement workshop, the world was shrinking to a single point of light and sound. Leonard stood in the center of his skeletal machine, the copper-lined coat a heavy, humming shroud around him. The air was thick, electric, the smell of ozone so strong it was a taste in the back of his throat. He was no longer a man. He was a component, a living filament in a circuit of desperation and hope.

The door at the top of the basement stairs burst open, the sound lost in a deafening crash of thunder. A figure stood there, silhouetted against the flickering, storm-wracked light of the alley. Water streamed from the brim of his hat, from the shoulders of his dark coat.

It was Inspector Welles.

He was not followed by a squad of uniformed officers. He was alone. He walked slowly down the wooden stairs, his face a mask of weary resolve. He looked at Leonard, at the strange, beautiful harp of a machine, at the wild, electric light in the professor's eyes. He looked like a man who had come to witness a miracle, or to stop one.

"It's over, Vaughn," Welles said, his voice tired but firm.

"There's nowhere left to run."

"I'm not running," Leonard said, his own voice sounding distant, resonant, as if it were already echoing from another place. "I'm going home."

"Home," Welles repeated, a sad, bitter smile on his lips.
"I've seen your inventions. The things you've given away. You could have been a king in this world. Instead, you build... this. A suicide machine."

"It's not a machine," Leonard said. "It's a memory. It's a song. And I am the only one who knows the melody."

Just then, a colossal fork of lightning struck a lamppost on the street outside. The world erupted in a flash of blue-white light and a sound like the sky being torn in half. The lights in the workshop and in the entire block died. They were plunged into a darkness so complete it was a physical presence.

But it was not a total darkness. A faint, ethereal light began to emanate from Leonard himself.

The copper threads in the coat began to glow, first with a soft, blue light, then with a brighter, whiter intensity. The machine, the amplifier, was drawing power not from the city, but from the storm itself, from the raw, untamed energy of the heavens, the earth's resonance, and it was channeling it all into the man who stood at its heart.

Welles stared, his professional skepticism, his devout rationality, his entire, ordered world dissolving in the face of the impossible thing happening before him. He saw the air around Leonard begin to shimmer, to bend. He saw the walls of the basement seem to waver, to become translucent. He was not just seeing a man in a machine; he was seeing a man in a machine. He was seeing the very fabric of reality coming undone.

"My God," Welles whispered, the words a prayer from a man who had forgotten how to pray.

Leonard closed his eyes. He let the storm flow into him. He thought of Mira, of her face in the collapsing light of his own time. He thought of Tesla, of his sad, wise eyes. He thought of Eddie, of his fierce, loyal heart. And he thought of Eleanor, of her quiet strength, of her impossible, selfless love. He gathered them all into his mind, the memories, the love, the loss. This was his frequency. This was his song.

He began to sing it.

He did not sing with his voice. He sang with his soul.

He broadcast his memory, his longing, his very being, his resonance, into the storm, into the machine, deep into the heart of time itself. The light around him intensified, becoming a blinding, unbearable sun. The hum rose to a single, pure, impossibly high note that was both sound and silence.

The building groaned, the foundations straining against the unnatural forces being unleashed in its heart. Cracks appeared in the walls. Dust and plaster rained down from the ceiling.

The world was coming apart.

Through the blinding light, Leonard saw a figure standing at the top of the stairs. It was Eleanor. She had not run. She was watching, her face illuminated by the impossible light, her eyes full of tears and a fierce, terrible pride. She was watching her love, her man from the future, go home.

He smiled at her, a final, silent thank you.
A final goodbye.

The world folded. It was not a gentle folding this time. It was a violent, tearing, screaming collapse of everything. Thunder and glass and light and the smell of rain and the memory of a woman's love all crashed together in a single, transcendent, and terrible moment.

Inspector Welles was thrown back against the far wall, the breath driven from his lungs. He shielded his eyes against the light, a light that seemed to burn not his skin, but his soul. He felt a wind, a hurricane, rush past him, a wind that was not made of air, but of time itself.

And then, as suddenly as it had begun, it was over.

The light was gone.

The sound was gone.

The man was gone.

The basement was a wreck. The machine was a twisted, blackened skeleton of wire and glass. The walls were cracked, and the ceiling was sagging. But the man, the source of the storm, had vanished. He had not run. He had not died. He had simply… ceased to be.

Welles, his ears ringing, his mind a shattered wreck, staggered to his feet. He looked at the empty space where Leonard had stood.

He had looked at a gaping hole torn in the fabric of his reality.

He was a man who had seen a miracle, and it did not fit on his report form.

He turned and walked slowly up the stairs, out into the rain-swept, silent street.

He saw a woman standing across the way, her face pale, her eyes fixed on the ruined building. He saw the love and the loss in her face. He knew who she was. He tipped his hat to her, a small, silent gesture of respect, of shared wonder, of a secret that would now bind them forever.

Then he turned and walked away, a man forever changed, a man who now knew that the world was a much stranger and more beautiful place than he had ever imagined.

From the alley, a small figure emerged. Eddie Rourke, soaked to the bone, his face a mixture of terror and awe. He looked at the ruined workshop, at the woman across the street, at the inspector walking away into the rain.

He looked up at the sky, where the storm was already beginning to break, and a few brave stars were starting to appear.

"He did it," the boy whispered to the empty, listening street.

"Professor Future. He went home."

Chapter 12

The Altered Return

He awoke to the taste of clean, recycled air and the gentle, familiar hum of a quantum processor. The transition was not a crash, but a soft, seamless fade, like waking from a long and vivid dream. The scent of ozone and coal smoke was gone, replaced by the sterile, comforting smell of his own time. He was lying on the floor of his laboratory, the cool, smooth surface a welcome balm against his cheek.

He was home.

He pushed himself up, his body aching with a strange, residual echo of the storm. The lab was intact. The copper coils gleamed on the walls, the processors blinked their silent, rhythmic lights. But something was different. The air of quiet desperation, of a secret, obsessive project hidden from the world, was gone. The room felt… brighter.

More open. More confident.

His eyes fell upon a set of blueprints, framed and hanging on the wall where the photograph of Tesla had once been. They were old; the paper was yellowed with age, and the ink had faded. They were the designs for a temporal resonance coil, a beautiful, impossible fusion of baroque coils and elegant quantum equations. In the bottom corner, two signatures, written in a confident, flowing script:

N. Tesla & L. Vass, 1909.

Leonard stared, his heart a wild, frantic drum. It had worked. He hadn't just returned. He had changed things. He had not erased the past, but rewritten it.

But then, his mind, that beautiful, terrible machine that could never rest, began to turn. He looked again at the blueprints, at the signature that was both a triumph and a puzzle.

N. Tesla & L. Vass, 1909.

The words were a key, but they unlocked a door he had not expected.

His mind raced as the equations and memories collided in a cascade of questions with no answers. If Tesla and he had worked together—truly worked together, long enough to co-sign blueprints, long enough to change the course of history—then that meant something fundamental had shifted in the timeline he remembered.

That meant he had never left the basement.

That meant he had never been caught by Inspector Welles, never been dragged away in chains, never made that desperate, final leap through the collapsing machine as the building burned around him.

That meant he had stayed.

He had finished the work.

But if he had stayed, if he had never been captured, then how had he gotten back, or to here?

How was he standing in this laboratory in 2069, remembering a past that, according to these blueprints, had never happened?

He felt a cold, creeping vertigo, the sensation of standing on the edge of a cliff that existed in his mind alone. Had he miscalculated the resonance equation? Did the lightning create too much power?

Had he made an error in the 3-6-9 sequence, the divine mathematics that Tesla had whispered to him in the candlelit dark of that lost workshop?

Had he not returned to his own timeline, but to a parallel one, a universe that was almost his, but not quite?

He looked around the laboratory, his eyes searching for something, anything, that felt wrong, that felt like a crack in the facade of reality. But everything was perfect. Too perfect. The equipment was more advanced than he remembered. The walls were cleaner. The air tasted different; sweeter, less heavy with the weight of a world powered by fossil fuels and compromise.

What is this future? Leonard thought the question felt like a cold stone in his chest.

Is this mine? Or have I stepped into someone else's dream?

He walked to the window, his legs unsteady, and looked out at the city. It was Orlando, yes. But it was an Orlando he did not quite recognize.

The buildings were taller, more graceful, their surfaces covered in a shimmering, living green. The sky was clearer.

The air, even through the sealed glass, seemed to hum with a clean, powerful energy. It was a world built on a foundation of Tesla's genius, not just as a footnote, but as a cornerstone.

It was beautiful. It was everything he had hoped for.
But it was not the world he had left.

He thought of Mira.

Dr. Mira Leung, his partner, his love, the woman who had believed in him when the rest of the world had called him mad. He thought of her face, her voice, the way she would tilt her head when she was working through a complex equation.

Did she exist here? And if she did, would she remember him? Would she remember the man who had vanished into the past, or would she only know the Leonard Vass of this timeline, the man who had co-authored the future with Nikola Tesla and had never left at all?

The thought was a knife, sharp and stiff. He had won. He had changed history. He had saved Tesla's legacy. But in doing so, had he erased himself?

Had he become a ghost in his own life, a man out of phase with his own reality?

He looked back at the blueprints, at the signature that was both his and not his.

N. Tesla & L. Vass, 1909.

It was a testament to a collaboration that he remembered, but that this world remembered differently. It was a bridge between two timelines, two possibilities, two versions of a man who had dared to argue with time itself.

And he realized, with a clarity that was both terrible and profound, that he might never know the answer. He might never know if he had returned home, or if he had simply found a better cage.

The only certainty was the uncertainty itself, the knowledge that time, like electricity, was not a river with a single current, but an ocean with infinite depths.

He had changed things. He had rewritten the past.

But in doing so, he had also rewritten himself. And now, standing in a laboratory that was both familiar and alien, he had to decide: was this the future he had fought for?
Or was it just another beautiful, impossible dream?

The question hung in the air, unanswered. And in the silence of the laboratory, the only sound was the soft, steady hum of a world powered by the genius of two men, separated by a century, united by a single, impossible equation.

N. Tesla & L. Vass, 1909.

The past was written.
The future was here.

But Leonard Vass, the man who had walked through time, was caught forever in the space between, a ghost in the machine of his own making.

Chapter 13

The Echo

He stumbled to the large window that looked out over the university campus. The world outside was not the world he had left. It was cleaner, brighter, more vibrant. The sky was a brilliant, cloudless blue, dotted not with the lazy, whispering drones of his memory, but with silent, graceful silver skiffs that moved with an effortless grace.

The architecture was a stunning blend of nature and technology, with buildings that seemed to grow out of the earth, covered in living green walls and shimmering solar panels that resembled the scales of a sleeping dragon. The air itself felt different, cleaner, charged with a quiet, joyful energy.

This was a world powered by clean, wireless energy. A world where Tesla's dreams had not been buried but celebrated. A world that had listened. A world that he, and a lonely ghost from 1909, had invented together.

On his workbench, where the failed interface had once sat, there was an old, yellowed envelope, sealed with a familiar wax stamp. His hands trembled as he picked it up.

It was addressed in Tesla's elegant, unmistakable hand:
To my friend from tomorrow.
He broke the seal.

The letter inside was brief, the ink faded but the words burning with a timeless fire.

"My dear friend," it began.

"If you are reading this, then our song has found its echo. You have returned to a world that you helped to create. Thank you. Thank you for not letting my dreams die in the darkness. Thank you for reminding me that the future is not something to be feared, but something to be invented. The world you have returned to is, I hope, a better one. But I know that all progress comes at a cost. I pray your cost was not too great. Live well in the world we built together, my friend. And sometimes, when you see a storm, think of the man who learned to speak its language. Your friend, Nikola."

The cost.

Leonard thought of Eleanor, of her quiet strength, of her face in the storm, of a love that he would now carry as a beautiful, secret wound for the rest of his life.

The cost had been great.

But the reward… the reward was all around him.

A voice, calm and melodic and achingly familiar, cut through his reverie.

"Professor Vass? Are you all right? I heard a noise."

He turned. Dr. Mira Leung stood in the doorway, her face a mask of polite, professional concern. She was the same, and yet, entirely different. The tired, weary lines around her eyes were gone. She stood with a new confidence, a new light in her eyes.

She was the woman he loved, the woman he had crossed a century to return to.

"Mira," he whispered, his voice thick with an emotion she could not possibly understand.

She gave him a strange, quizzical look. "I'm sorry, have we met? I'm Dr. Leung. I'm the new head of the Temporal Physics department. I was just coming to introduce myself. I'm a great admirer of your work, of course. Your grandfather's work, I should say."

His grandfather. Of course. Leonard Vass, 1909. The man who had appeared from nowhere, who had partnered with the great Tesla, who had helped to change the world.

He was a legacy now. A historical footnote.

The heartbreak was a quiet, subtle thing, a pain so sharp and so deep that it was almost beautiful. He remembered her. He remembered their late nights in the lab, their shared dreams, the feel of her hand in his. He remembered a love that, in this new, better world, had never existed.

She saw the look in his eyes, the strange, profound sadness, and a flicker of something passed over her face. A shadow of a memory that wasn't hers. A strange sense of déjà vu.

"I'm sorry," she said, a faint blush on her cheeks. "You just… you feel very familiar. It feels as if I've known you my whole life."

She was the echo the future leaves behind when love travels backward.

Leonard smiled, a sad, gentle smile that did not quite reach his eyes.

"It's a pleasure to meet you, Dr. Leung. I have a feeling we're going to do great things together."

The final image of his long, strange journey was this: Leonard Vass, a professor in a world he had helped to build, standing in a classroom filled with bright, eager faces, teaching the science of time.

On the wall behind him hung the framed blueprints, a testament to a friendship that had transcended a century.

He was a hero. He was a ghost.

He was a man with a divided heart, a man who remembered two women, two loves, two lives. He had saved the future, but he had lost his own past.

He was the man who could speak to time, but who was now, and forever, alone in his own memory.

The world was a better place.
The world was resonant.

But the conductor of the orchestra would carry the sad, beautiful music of his sacrifice in the silence of his own heart, for all of time.

TO BE CONTINUED...

AUTHOR'S NOTES

This is the work of creative fiction. I've always daydreamed about going back to the future using a futuristic device and bringing them back to this current timeline. This story developed from that daydream; to going back in time and getting stuck there. Nikola Tesla dialed in to the earth's natural resonance, Wardenclyffe and the Philadelphia Experiment fit neatly into the time machine aspect of this story.

I've often wondered what this world would have become if Tesla won the energy battle; resonant energy for all, for free.

ABOUT THE AUTHOR

www.lennylegermedia.com

LEONARD
AND THE
CLOCKWORK
FUTURE

LENNY LEGER

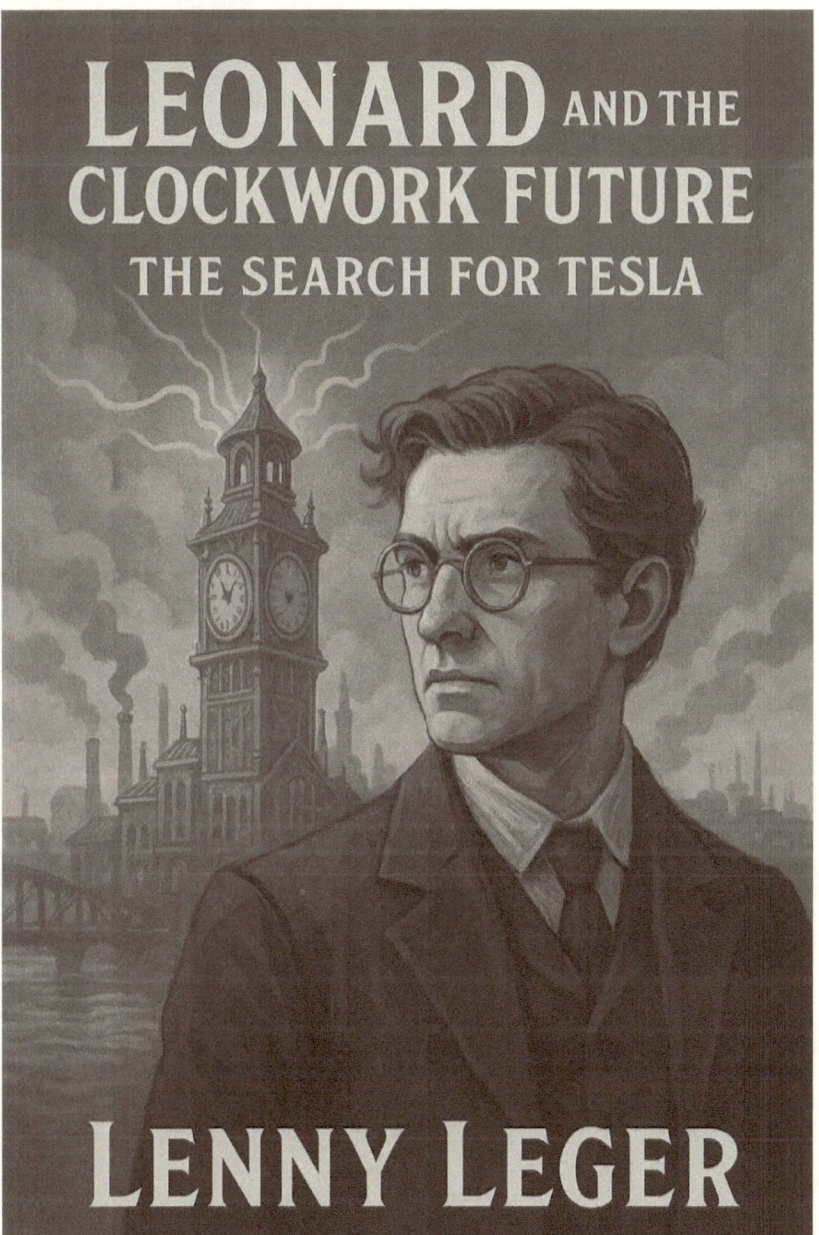

LEONARD AND THE
CLOCKWORK FUTURE
THE SEARCH FOR TESLA

LENNY LEGER

www.ingramcontent.com/pod-product-compliance
Lightning Source LLC
Chambersburg PA
CBHW020545130626
46552CB00007B/2761